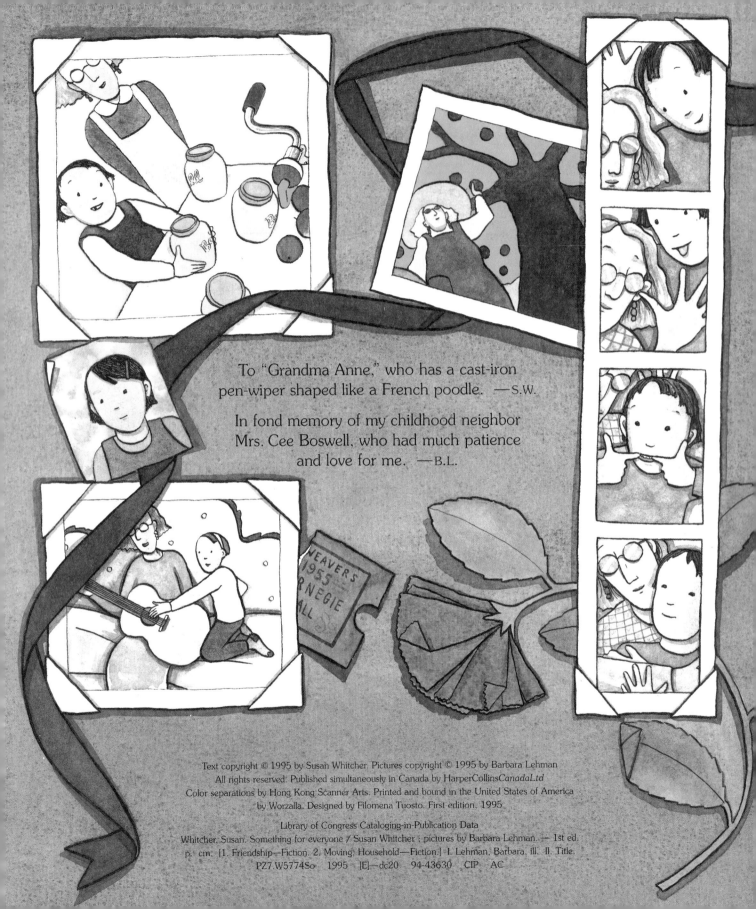

To "Grandma Anne," who has a cast-iron
pen-wiper shaped like a French poodle. —S.W.

In fond memory of my childhood neighbor
Mrs. Cee Boswell, who had much patience
and love for me. —B.L.

Text copyright © 1995 by Susan Whitcher. Pictures copyright © 1995 by Barbara Lehman.
All rights reserved. Published simultaneously in Canada by HarperCollins Canada Ltd.
Color separations by Hong Kong Scanner Arts. Printed and bound in the United States of America
by Worzalla. Designed by Filomena Tuosto. First edition, 1995.
Library of Congress Cataloging-in-Publication Data
Whitcher, Susan. Something for everyone / Susan Whitcher ; pictures by Barbara Lehman. — 1st ed.
p. cm. [1. Friendship—Fiction. 2. Moving, Household—Fiction.] I. Lehman, Barbara, ill. II. Title.
PZ7.W5774So 1995 [E]—dc20 94-43630 CIP AC

# Something for Everyone

SUSAN WHITCHER

Pictures by BARBARA LEHMAN

FARRAR, STRAUS AND GIROUX • NEW YORK

**G**reat-aunt Elsie Appelbaum was going away.
"For good," she said. "I'm going to live in a
warm country beside the sea."

She sold her house and furniture. She gave
away her special things.
  "To remember me by," Great-aunt Elsie
Appelbaum told her friend, little Tilda-next-door.

Great-aunt Elsie left something for everyone.
So everyone came, cousins and aunts, great-
nieces and great-great-step-nephews-in-law.
But no one was satisfied.

To Aunt Ada Sauerwein she left her guitar.

"You lucker!" cried Tilda.

Aunt Ada straightened her rings and wrinkled her lips. "I never play anymore," she snapped.

For Cousin Rob Barger there was a pair of fur-lined boots.

"She won't need these where she went to," Tilda said with a sigh, touching the fur with the tip of her finger.

"Who got the set of eight bone-handled cheese forks?" demanded Cousin Rob.

"Don't tell me she sold the camelback settee!" grumbled Aunt Ada Sauerwein.

"It's not fair," complained Great-niece Mona Wetmore-Draine. Her name was on a cardboard box in the kitchen.

"Oh, look," said Tilda. "It's the special apple peeler! She always let me turn the crank when we made applesauce."

"Applesauce!" Mona sniffed. "I told her to get me a powder-blue cashmere twin set, size sixteen."

"Someone will have to clear up all this trash," declared Cousin Rob.

Aunt Ada gathered up her purse and her gloves. "It's very inconvenient," she said.

So Tilda collected the things that nobody wanted and put them together. She put them together in a special way, because they were the special things that belonged to Great-aunt Elsie Appelbaum.

When she was finished, she turned the crank.
The guitar began to buzz. Tilda climbed aboard.
"You can't do that," whined Mona Wetmore-Draine.
"Stop that at once!" barked Cousin Rob Barger.
"How dare you?" shrieked Aunt Ada Sauerwein.
But Tilda dared. "Goodbye," she called. "Goodbye!"

Tilda flew high and fast and breathless with wind and wonder. The guitar strings thrummed from the rush of flying. But close behind her loomed a cloud, a great dim billowy cloud of powder-blue fog.

Fingers of fog reached and clung to Tilda's machine. Rain thudded on the guitar. The wings sagged.

They struggled to flap, but the rain beat them
down. Tilda dropped through branches that
snapped and snatched at her.

Then she found herself in the wild woods where
the ada-birds lurked. And it was almost dark. She
went on tiptoe. The ada-birds followed. Their eyes
were bright as pins. So Tilda sang to them.

She sang "Red River Valley" and "You Are My
Sunshine." She picked out chords on the guitar the
way Great-aunt Elsie Appelbaum showed her, and
banged the strings when she forgot the chords.

The ada-birds flew away screeking.

Tilda marched through the dark woods singing
loud. Ahead, the branches thinned, and stars were
shining. There was the sea. Tilda set sail by
starlight.

But at dawn the sea bristled with pirate ships.
The pirates gnashed their teeth and brandished
wicked bone-handled cheese forks.

"Give up!" they bellowed. "We've got you
surrounded!"

Tilda was too quick for them. Her cannons
boomed out. Apples of green and red put a stop to
those forks. Great-aunt Elsie's special apple peeler
churned the waves like sauce.

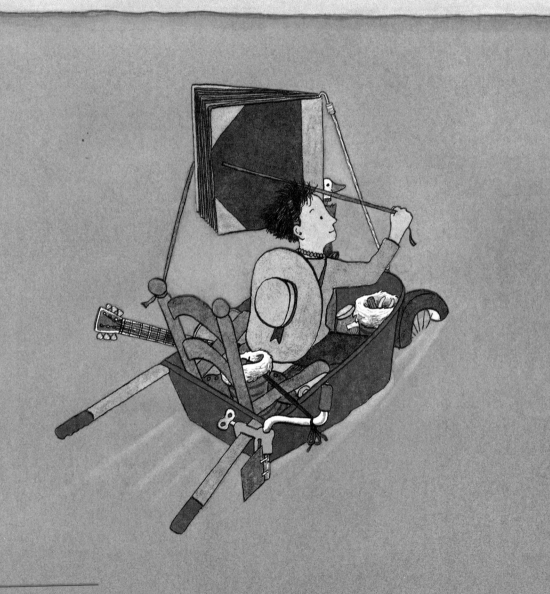

Soon the pirates were left far behind, and the shore was near.

On the beach was a tea table where Great-aunt Elsie Appelbaum sat under a purple umbrella.

"Thank heavens you came!" exclaimed Great-aunt Elsie Appelbaum. "I left the last three cookies on the plate for you."

"Oh, good," said Tilda.